THE
HOLLYHONK GARDENS
OF GNEEDLE AND GNIBB

A BOOK ABOUT
FORGIVING

Michael P. Waite
Illustrated by Jill Colbert Trousdale

Chariot Books™
David C. Cook Publishing Co.

For Nathan and Heather, my two favorite
gnomes! MPW

To my families, where only a little forgiving
is needed. JCT

Chariot Books™ is an imprint of David C. Cook Publishing Co.
David C. Cook Publishing Co., Elgin, Illinois 60120
David C. Cook Publishing Co., Weston, Ontario
Nova Distribution Ltd., Newton Abbot, England
THE HOLLYHONK GARDENS OF GNEEDLE AND GNIBB
© 1993 by Michael P. Waite for text and illustrations

Designed by Studio North
First Printing, 1992
Printed in the United States of America
97 96 95 94 93 5 4 3 2
Library of Congress Cataloging-in-Publication Data
Waite, Michael P., 1960-
    The Hollyhonk gardens of Gneedle and Gnibb / Michael P. Waite; illustrated by Jill Colbert Trousdale.
    p. cm. — (Building Christian character)
    Summary: Petty arguments almost cost two gnomes their friendship and their beautiful gardens.
    ISBN 0-7814-0034-1
    [1. Forgiveness—Fiction. 2. Friendship—Fiction. 3. Gardening—Fiction. 4. Gnomes—Fiction. 5. Stories in rhyme.]
I. Trousdale, Jill, ill. II. Title. III. Series: Waite, Michael P., 1960- Building Christian character.
PZ8.3.W136HO 1992   91-38876
[E]—dc20   CIP   AC

In Green Gully Grove,
In a tiny log home,
Lived a good little gardener
Named Gneedle the gnome.

4

Just over the clover,
A frog-hop away,
Lived her friend Gnibb
In a cottage of hay.

And most every day
The two gnomes would stay
Outside in their gardens working away.

Gneedle grew flowers that lit up at night—
Flickerworts, Blinkins, and oh, what a sight!
Glowroots which gleamed with a glimmering light!

Gnibb grew a garden of musical flowers—
Drumbleweeds, Boombas, great tooting towers,
And Hollyhonks humming to wee morning hours!

7

Gneedle helped Gnibb
With his seeding and weeding

And borrowed his tools
(Just some things she was needing)—
A small pair of clippers,
Some gardening slippers,
A shovel, a pitchfork, a hose and a hoe,
And some Zoomabloom Dust,
Which made anything grow.

Then in the evening,
On every clear night,
They'd sit by their gardens
And watch with delight

As the Blinkins and Flickerworts
Lit up so bright,
And the Drumbleweeds drumbled,
The big Boombas rumbled,
And Hollyhonks pleasantly
Murmured and mumbled.

Because of the beautiful
Sparkle and sound,
Not a thistle nor thorn
Could grow in the ground.

One summer's day, Gneedle needed a pail,
So she borrowed the bucket Gnibb kept on a nail.
And as she was crossing the garden toward home
THWAK! went a rake
As it smacked the poor gnome!

"OUCH!" hollered Gneedle, glaring at Gnibb,
Rubbing her noggin, her nose, and her rib.
"You left out this rake, just so I would trip!
Now look at my nose and my poor puffy lip!"

"It's all your own fault!" Gnibb snorted at Gneedle,
"And put back my bucket, you burgaling beetle!"

13

They stared and they glared for a minute or more,
Then they both stomped away,
Stormed inside,
Slammed their doors!

"If that's what he wants,"
Gneedle snorted, "Then fine!
But until he is sorry, he's no friend of mine!"

Later that night, she heard pounding outside,
So she looked out the window—
And guess what she spied?
Gnibb! He was building a big wooden fence!
She thought for a moment . . . and then it made sense!
Gnibb was so mad
And his temper so bad
He was *fencing out* Gneedle—
What a crafty old cad!

Gneedle could hear all his Hollyhonks hooting,
O how she hated that tweeting and tooting!
So promptly she gathered some mortar and stone,
And got to work building a wall of her own!

For three weary weeks,
Those two sniveling sneaks
Hoisted and hammered, with dirt on their cheeks.
And when they were done, they looked up in the sky—
His fence and her wall stood a hundred feet high!
Not a sight nor a sound could ever get by!

Gneedle plopped down on her doorstep and scowled.
"I won't have to look at him now!" Gneedle growled.

Then she glared at the ground
And bitterly frowned,
For all of her flowers had withered and browned—
All but one sprout,
Just a leaf peeking out,
And that would die too,
Gneedle hadn't a doubt.

So she shuffled to bed,
With an ache in her head,
And while she was sleeping and silently weeping
A thicket of thistles
Came quietly creeping—
Bitter-Brush Briar
And Nip-Nasty Nettle
Began to take root, and to shoot, and to settle!

When Gneedle awoke they had grown up the wall.
They had sprawled,
They had crawled,
They had covered it all!
They filled up the sky
With their thistles and thorns,
And the sun could not shine
Through those horrible horns!

Gneedle sat down on her porch in the gloom
And wished she could hear
Just one Boomba plant boom.
She thought about Gnibb,
How they used to have fun,
How they used to have gardens
That grew in the sun.
She wondered,
And wondered,
"O what have I done?"

She noticed Gnibb's stuff—
All that stuff in a stack—
All the stuff that she'd borrowed
And never brought back!

"It's my fault!" she sniffled.
"I've lost my best friend!
If he knew I was sorry
This whole mess would end.
But the wall is too high
With those thorns in the sky . . ."
And she sat on her doorstep and started to cry.

And that's when she saw it
All covered with rust,
Gnibb's little can full of Zoomabloom Dust!
Her one tiny chance
That the last of her plants
Would live to grow up and to glow and to dance!

So she ran to her garden,
All buried in briars,
She propped up her Glowroot
With branches and wires,
And sprinkled the Zoomabloom over the ground,
She weeded and watered and stirred it around.
Through the hot hazy day
And the chilly night air,
She showered that flower with love and with care,

Till sorrow and sleepiness clouded her eyes,
And she drifted in dreams of forgotten blue skies.

She awoke to the shock of a bright yellow glow—
She climbed to her feet, startled and slow.
And there in the air
Her flower so fair
Was shining and shimmering, bright as a prayer!

The sky filled with creaking
And crackling and crumbling!
The briars were dying!
The fences were tumbling!
With one mighty CRASH!
The whole wall toppled down
And tangled together with weeds on the ground!

Out of the smoke, with a shout and a smile,
Came jolly old Gnibb,
Hopping over the pile!

"Gnibb!" Gneedle cried,
With her arms opened wide,
"Won't you forgive all my meanness and pride?"

And as they forgave one another with hugs,
The sand and the grass
And the thorn-eating bugs
Swallowed up all of the Bitter-Brush weeds,
The roots and the shoots,
And even the seeds!

29

So now in the forests
Of Green Gully Grove,
You'll find our two gnomes
By their homes in the cove.
Their Hollyhonks, Boombas, and Blinkins are growing,
And hooting and tooting,
                   And gleaming and glowing!

But there's not a Bitter-Brush Briar nearby,
And if you'll look closely, you'll figure out why!